THE JURASSIC COAST

BOOK FIVE

STEPHANIE BAUDET

Published by Sweet Cherry Publishing Limited
Unit 36, Vulcan House
Vulcan Road
Leicester, LE5 3EF
United Kingdom

www.sweetcherrypublishing.com

First published in the UK in 2016
2020 edition

ISBN: 978-1-78226-269-5

The Dinosaur Detectives: The Jurassic Coast

Printed and bound in India
I.IPP001

CHAPTER ONE

The egg was oval, like a really big Easter egg, although much heavier. Matt Sharp was used to the weight now, and it was only for a moment. As the misty spinning sensation took over, he became unaware of how heavy the egg felt.

The scene opened up in front of him and he forgot about the presence of his dad and his cousin, Jo. He was back in the Jurassic period – the time of dinosaurs, and he was standing on a pebbly beach with high rocky cliffs to his left. The sea swirled in and out, much as it does in modern times, and Matt noticed that he now had the ability to hear! He could hear the waves lapping and the trickle of the water against the pebbles.

With each of his visions he gained more abilities, and he wondered briefly what that meant and where it would lead him next!

A heavy crunching noise to his left made him look quickly, and there, only a short distance away, stood a medium-sized dinosaur, about four metres long, foraging amongst the pebbles. Of course, it was unaware of Matt's presence, but his new ability to hear his surroundings made it seem much more real. For the first time he felt a little nervous, although he knew that he was safe.

As he watched, the creature tugged at a piece of green fern growing between some rocks,

then lifted its small head and munched away. *A herbivore then*, Matt thought, and somehow it was a relief. It was a strange-looking dinosaur, with its small head and short neck. It had a heavy body with armoured plates embedded in its back.

Matt had no idea where he was in the world, but he knew that in the time he was seeing now, the world was far different from what it was like in the present day. All the continents had been joined in one large land mass called Pangaea until they began to drift apart about 175 million years ago, in the early to mid-Jurassic period.

He became aware of someone talking as the vision of the dinosaur became hazy and he came back to the present.

'What is it?' His dad was like an excited child, almost jumping up and down in anticipation.

Jo, Matt's cousin, watched him too; she almost seemed to be holding her breath.

'I think it was a scelidosaurus, like you said, Dad. It was about four metres long and had a small head and a big body with armour-plating. It was eating greenery on a seashore.'

'And did it have …?' His dad pointed to his own ears and Matt smiled.

'Yes, Dad, it had little three-pronged horns behind its ears.'

His dad pushed a piece of paper and a pencil towards him across the kitchen table, and Matt began to draw what he'd seen while it was still fresh in his mind. He could draw quite well but not nearly as well as his dad, who was well-known around the world for his dinosaur artwork. *He is a fantastic palaeo-artist as well as a renowned palaeontologist*, Matt thought proudly.

As he finished his sketch his dad said, 'Well, it's a coincidence, but the scelidosaurus was found recently in Lyme Regis, in Dorset, and that's where we're going soon too.'

'On a dig?'

Mr Sharp shook his head. 'A distant uncle has died and we are going to clear his old house ready for sale, so no digging for me, but you two can go fossil-hunting. It's not called the Jurassic Coast for nothing!'

CHAPTER TWO

'I've heard of the Jurassic Coast,' said Jo.

Matt rolled his eyes. He still wasn't sure what to make of Jo. At times he didn't mind her company, but at other times she just irritated him.

'It's where a famous fossil collector called Mary Anning discovered several dinosaur skeletons in the early 19th century,' said Matt's dad. 'She found the very first ichthyosaur when she was just twelve years old, in 1811. Of course, no one knew what it was. She thought it was a crocodile.'

Jo smiled.

'Most people thought that nothing was more than about six thousand years old and that these creatures had perished in the great Flood,' Matt's dad continued. 'To suggest that anything was older went against the religious beliefs of the time, and was considered heresy.'

'She was a few years out then!' said Matt with a chuckle.

Dad smiled. 'The museum in Lyme Regis is built on the site of the house where she was born,' he went on. 'You'll hear a lot about her when we get there.'

Matt was looking forward to the trip, although not as much as the actual expeditions he was now allowed to go on with his dad. 'When you're twelve,' Dad had always said, and last year it had happened: Matt was finally able to join his dad on any trips that happened during school holidays. Now he had been on four expeditions to various exciting parts of the world. The one sore point was Jo. Because both her parents were doctors and couldn't take time off to look after her, she always came too, even though she was only eleven. It was not exactly what Matt had envisaged for all those years: he'd looked forward to it being just him and Dad together, unearthing dinosaur fossils, and especially eggs. Those were his dad's speciality. Matt was still uncertain about Jo. At times though, he had to admit, it had been good to have her around. She was intelligent, and no wimp. The other expeditions had certainly been exciting as well as dangerous, and then there was Frank Hellman, Dad's rival, invariably turning up to try to steal the eggs and claim the prestige and the money he got for selling to private collectors.

On their first day in Lyme Regis they all went to the museum: Mum, Dad, Jo, Matt, and his younger sister, Beth, aged ten, who had no interest whatsoever in dinosaurs, for which Matt was thankful.

In the afternoon they went on the Mary Anning guided tour and learnt that, as Dad had said, the museum was built on the site of her birthplace. It had once been a poor part of town and the area in front of the museum had been called Cockmoil Square, where a prison had stood at that time. It was very close to the sea and when there was a storm or a particularly high tide, the house flooded, especially the basement where Mary Anning cleaned the ammonites and other fossils she found, ready for sale to visitors as 'curiosities'. It was where she laid out her big finds, too, before setting them in plaster of Paris for safe transportation to buyers in London. Nowadays though, there was a sea wall to prevent flooding.

The visit fired up Matt's enthusiasm, although

he was more interested in the larger prehistoric animals than the ammonites. Nevertheless, he knew that they were here to clear the house, and the next day they started that in earnest.

Their distant uncle, it seemed, had done very little to the house he had lived in for most of his life. It was old and decrepit. The outside was an eyesore and spoilt the look of the street. Because it was in the middle of the town it had no garden, and the front door was almost straight onto the road. There was a very short path with a couple of rocks marking a sort of gateway off the pavement, and then two steps up to the front door.

The bedrooms were not too bad and were habitable, although Matt's family had brought camp beds and sleeping bags.

'I can't believe anyone could live like this,' said Matt's mum, looking round at the peeling paint and stacks of rubbish. 'Who is going to buy it?'

'Oh, a property developer, I expect,' said Dad. 'It's right in the town and has a sea view.'

'I should think that everyone has a sea view here,' said Mum. 'The whole town is built on a slope! Come on, you kids. You can help. Where do you want to start?'

'Can't we go fossil-hunting?' asked Jo.

Ooh, that's pushing it, thought Matt, but Mum just smiled.

'No, Jo, not today. We need help here. This is why we are down here after all; it's not a fossil-hunting expedition. You can go tomorrow, all right? But first we must make some inroads into this.'

Jo glanced at Matt, who raised his eyebrows. What did she expect?

'Why don't you explore the cellar?' said Dad. 'That might be your sort of place.' He looked at Beth. 'You can go too, Beth.'

Beth shook her head vehemently. 'No thanks. It's definitely not *my* sort of place!'

There was coal in the cellar, as one might expect. There was a lifetime's worth of rubbish there too. Also an old bike, stacks of mouldy cardboard boxes, and rusty garden tools, despite the fact that there was only a patio at the back and no garden.

'Where do we start?' said Matt with a sigh.

Dad had hired a skip so they began taking all the items they could carry up the cellar steps and out to it. The cardboard boxes were full of old newspapers and magazines, but a glance at them showed that they were just daily papers and of no interest to anyone, so out they went. Why did people hoard all these useless things?

By lunchtime they had cleared quite a large section. Matt was just stretching his arms before going to see what there was to eat, when he saw something curious.

There was an irregularity in the brick wall in front of him, which wasn't strange in such an old house: one of the bricks looked loose and was sticking out a little. Matt reached forward and waggled it a little to free it. To his surprise, it came out easily.

In the cavity behind the brick, there was a roll of paper. He reached in and carefully pulled it

out. He could see that it was old, but it wasn't mouldy like the cardboard boxes had been.

'What is it?' said Jo from the other side of the room.

Matt smiled to himself; you couldn't keep anything from Jo.

Before he could have a good look at the paper though, Beth's voice called down the stairs, 'Lunch, you guys!'

Matt replaced the paper and the brick and looked at Jo. He didn't need to tell her not to say anything.

CHAPTER THREE

Once lunch was over and they were back down in the cellar, Jo leaned over Matt's shoulder eagerly as he carefully unrolled the paper. It was old and fragile.

'What is it?'

'It's a drawing of a dinosaur,' said Matt, realising that he was doing the same thing that sometimes irritated him about Jo – he was stating the obvious. The picture was an ink drawing with a brownish wash over it. He wasn't sure what type of dinosaur it was though. He peered at the writing at the bottom right of the picture.

'H. De la Beche,' he read. 'I wonder who he was?'

'A good artist,' said Jo. 'Just like Uncle Alan. 'Do you think he found this dinosaur fossil here?'

Matt shrugged and then shook his head to try

to get rid of the feeling of strange fuzziness that had washed over him. Maybe the air down here was a bit stale. He should go upstairs for some fresh air.

'What's the matter?' asked Jo, but Matt couldn't answer. The cellar was already fading out and a new scene was developing. He was in the same cellar, but it was different. It was tidier, and lit only with a spirit lamp. What was going on? This shouldn't be happening! The visions, until now, had only happened when he was holding a dinosaur egg.

Two figures were materialising. The woman was dressed in a long, worn-looking black skirt, and she was pulling off her bonnet and shawl. At the same time she seemed to be having an argument with the man standing in front of her. He was better dressed, in breeches and boots and a greatcoat.

'It *is* a fossil, I am sure of it,' she said.

'Bones are long, Mary. Even the skulls of these creatures are not round. It is just a rock, and you must not risk your life and limb trying to reach it.'

She was quiet for a moment and then said, 'You are right about that last part, Henry. It is just so high up that there is no means of excavating it.

Perhaps with the next storm it will be dislodged.'

He turned to her and smiled. 'Not that you are a stranger to the dangers of fossil-hunting. You risk injury or worse every time you forage around the cliffs.' He reached into a pocket of his greatcoat. 'Is this how you visualise your latest find?'

She took the paper and studied it. Then she smiled and nodded. 'You have given it such life, Henry. It almost seems to leap from the page.'

'Matt! Are you all right?'

Matt felt Jo tugging at his arm as the figures faded, and suddenly he was back in the cellar with her.

'I saw two people,' he said. 'I'm sure it was Mary Anning. I recognised her from the museum. She was with a man she called Henry.' He held up the drawing. 'He was the artist and he was giving her this. She was talking about something high up in the cliff that she couldn't reach. She thought it was a fossil but he thought it was probably only a round rock.'

'That must be what the map shows,' said Jo, pointing to the back of the paper. She looked at him again. 'Your psychic powers are increasing.'

For some reason what she said irritated Matt. He'd never thought of his visions as being psychic. They had only happened when he'd held the dinosaur eggs before. Now he couldn't understand why he was seeing people, although they *were* connected to dinosaurs.

'What map?' He turned over the drawing. On the back of the sheet was a sketch of the coastline and cliffs. There was a cross somewhere in the middle of the cliff.

'Yeah! Of course!' Matt felt a bubble of excitement inside him, which smoothed out his irritation. 'We should see if we can locate it.'

'Matt, Mary Anning lived a long time ago. We should find out more about her first. Maybe she did excavate whatever it was,' Jo replied.

'We should make a copy of this,' said Matt. 'It might be valuable. Dad will be interested.'

But Matt and Jo decided not to tell Matt's dad about the drawing straight away. Not until they'd explored it further.

A quick internet search reminded them that Mary Anning had lived from 1799 to 1847 and was considered the greatest fossil hunter ever. Her family had been very poor so, as a child, she collected the numerous 'curiosities' that could be found on the shore and sold them to the many holiday makers who flocked to Lyme Regis during the summer months to bathe in the health-giving waters. These fossils were mostly belemnites and ammonites, but when she was twelve Mary and her brother, Joseph, had uncovered an ichthyosaurus, which they had thought was a crocodile.

Later she'd made even greater finds and sold them to prominent geologists. The name Henry De la Beche came up amongst them. In time, Mary became very knowledgeable about fossils and was regularly consulted by eminent scientists. Because she was a woman, though, she had never been admitted to the Geological Society.

Jo snorted, stabbing a finger at the screen. 'They didn't let women become members until 1919! She wasn't even allowed in the building. Poor Mary!'

'So we don't know what she found in the cliff or whether she ever excavated it,' said Matt. 'But we might as well try to locate it on the map. It's something to do.'

Being Easter, it wasn't warm enough to swim in the sea, so they planned to go the next day.

But in the meantime, two things happened.

CHAPTER FOUR

A storm blew up during the night and continued well into the morning. No-one was going anywhere, especially onto the beach with its pounding waves and unstable cliffs. Matt and Jo were kept busy helping pack stuff in boxes to go to a charity shop while Mum and Dad continued to clean and wash the rooms, one by one.

The old house creaked and whined; the loose sash windows rattled so violently that when there was a knock on the door, no-one was quite sure that it was a knock. When they heard it again, Matt heard his dad sigh and walk to the door. As soon as he'd opened it, it was flung back with a crash and someone made a noisy entrance, ignoring Mr Sharp's protestations. A gust of wind blew into the hallway and, somewhere inside the house, a door slammed.

Matt recognised who it was straightaway. A big man with a closely shaven head swaggered into the room.

It was Frank Hellman himself.

Matt and Jo jumped to their feet. The last time they had actually seen this man had been in the Amazon rainforest, when he and his men had threatened them if they didn't hand over the fossilised eggs they had uncovered. Luckily at that point some loggers working nearby had saved the day.

'I don't remember inviting you in, Hellman. What do you want? What are you doing here?' Dad's face looked like thunder.

Mum and Beth had followed him into the room, hearing all the noise. Matt noticed that his mum's face looked strained with worry.

Frank Hellman took his time to answer, aware of the effect he was having. Then he looked around and smiled. 'I would have thought you could afford better than this, Sharp. I was curious. I heard you were here but wasn't aware of any significant finds. I just had to come and ask.'

'This is not an expedition, Hellman, so you've wasted your time. It's personal business, please leave.'

Frank Hellman fixed his stare on Matt and Jo. 'I expect you'll be out there picking up ammonites as soon as the weather improves. Or aren't they good enough for you? But if you do go, watch your backs. If you find anything worthwhile, you'd better save it for me.'

'Don't you dare threaten my kids! You parasite! Leave now before I call the police.'

Frank Hellman threw back his head and laughed. 'I can afford to wait, Sharp,' he said. 'My little enterprises are like gold mines – or should I say opal mines?' He was reminding them of their last expedition in Australia.

And illegal logging, thought Matt, glancing at Jo. She'd got really steamed up about that.

'Your father would turn in his grave if he could see you now, Hellman,' said Dad.

The man's face turned livid with anger. 'A grave *your* father put him in!' He turned and strode out, and Dad shut the door firmly after him.

'Don't be too worried, kids,' he said, returning to the living room. 'He just wants to scare you. I doubt that he'll hang around here long now he knows that we're not fossil-hunting.'

Matt wondered what he had meant by their granddad putting Frank's father in his grave, but he knew better than to ask, and Jo was learning to hold her tongue, too.

The sea still looked grey and choppy and there was a cool breeze, but Matt and Jo had had enough of being indoors after the previous day and they wanted to explore the beach. It was just before ten o'clock and after a lecture from Matt's dad about the dangers of incoming tides, and of landslides after rain, they left the house. He hadn't mentioned Frank Hellman, but Matt was fairly certain they weren't in danger from him. Not real danger.

'Stay where there are other people,' Dad had said. 'Away from the base of the cliff.'

The trouble was that there weren't many people about. There was only one lady, who was walking her dog, and a couple of teenagers foraging in the wet sand.

Further along, Matt could see one or two people obviously looking for fossils. Maybe when the sun was higher the warmth would bring more people out. After a storm was the best time to look for fossils.

Matt took the copy of the map out of his jeans pocket and unfolded it. At least he wouldn't have any visions holding this version.

Even without the vision, he could imagine the prehistoric creatures roaming the shore and swarming the ocean. The scelidosaurus that he'd seen in his last vision would have measured up to four metres long and weighed 250 kilograms.

The ichthyosaurus that Mary and her brother had found when she was twelve was a strong swimmer well-adapted to life in the sea, although it still needed to surface periodically to breathe

air. They could grow up to nine metres long and had sharp teeth and long claws. Not something you would want to meet while swimming.

Matt looked at the sea, imagining those long heads with their big eyes breaking the surface for air.

'Matt! Are you having a vision, or what?' Jo turned to look back at her cousin.

Matt grinned. 'Not in the way you mean. I was just imagining life here in prehistoric times. It's hard to think in millions of years, isn't it?'

Jo nodded and moved away from the patch of pebbles and rocks she'd been inspecting. 'Look, I found a small ammonite.' She opened her palm.

'It's a start,' said Matt.

The map seemed to lead them away from the town, and soon there were cliffs on their left. Church Cliffs, the map said, and then Black Ven. There was fresh rubble showing that the storm had brought down some of the cliff face. Signs warned people to stay clear of the foot of the cliffs. One of the signs had been knocked down by falling earth and he could just see a corner of it sticking out.

Jo pointed to a pile of rubbish that had been thrown up against a large rock by the sea. 'Just look at that!' she said indignantly.

Matt smiled to himself. So this was to be Jo's project this time. He did care about these things, but he didn't have the passion Jo had. 'Don't touch it, Jo.'

'I'm not going to.' She looked at him. 'Do you think I'm mad or something? I'll come back with some gloves and a bag.' She tutted again, looking at the drinks cans and empty polystyrene food containers.

Count me out, thought Matt. He looked at the map again and a feeling of despondency came over him.

'Do you think this is a waste of time, Jo?' he said. 'We are following a two hundred year old map that might be someone's idea of a joke. I mean, X marks the spot. It's like a corny story. Even if it is genuine, look how the cliffs can change in one day! Imagine how much it has changed in two centuries!'

Jo shook her head. 'It doesn't matter, does it? It's fun, and we've nothing else to do. It beats clearing out the house. There are lots of fossils here, just not the sort we're usually interested in.'

Matt's mood lightened. 'But you never know. There might be. And we're nearly there.'

He had given her the map and she glanced down at it. 'The trouble is, the X seems to be *in* the cliff.'

Matt looked up at the cliffs and nodded. 'That's it then. It would be really daft to ignore all these signs.'

'Don't you think that the storm has washed down anything that's loose?'

'It's *after* the rain that it slips too. It takes time for the rain to seep through the ground.'

She nodded and walked on, picking her way over the rocky beach, kicking at more litter as she went.

The cliff face to their left gradually went from looking quite soft and crumbly to more solid-looking rock. In fact, the top was a lot lower now, barely ten metres.

'It's about here.'

They both stopped and looked at the cliff.

Matt knew they should heed the signs, though he was worried that Jo would want to keep going: she could be foolhardy at times. Even though the cliffs were not high, rocks falling from just three metres could quite easily kill someone.

'Matt! Did you hear that?' Jo was standing still. 'Something's crying.'

'Seagulls,' said Matt. There were plenty of them about, swooping and crying.

She shook her head. 'I don't think so. Do you think someone is trapped?'

'By what? There haven't been any rock falls here.' He listened, too, and didn't hear anything at first. He shook his head, ready to be firm and say they should turn back.

But then he did hear it, faintly, carried by the wind. A thin, plaintive cry, like that of a small child.

CHAPTER FIVE

But it could still be seagulls.

'You heard it, didn't you?' said Jo. 'We can't leave it. What if it is a child, Matt?'

'If it was a child, people would be out looking for it.' Matt tried to reason with himself, but somehow he knew he couldn't just walk away.

The cry came again, between the cries of the gulls. There was no doubt about it; this sound *was* different.

Jo began to stride towards the cliffs in a determined way, her hair flying about in the brisk breeze. She pushed it behind her ears, giving Matt a glimpse at the dogged set of her face.

He ran after her. 'Well, be careful!'

Matt noticed that there *was* some rubble from earlier cliff erosion, but also some scrubby bushes growing at the base of the cliff, showing, he hoped, that there hadn't been a landslide for some time. On the other hand, maybe they hadn't had a storm like last night for some time either.

He pushed on, trying to keep up with Jo. The cry came again, closer, behind the bushes.

'Matt! There's a cave!'

He pushed aside the branches, and there was Jo, standing at the entrance of a cave. The opening was quite high – something like four metres he guessed, but not only was it hidden by the bushes, there was a twist in the rock face that made it impossible to see from the beach. You had to get right up close before you noticed it.

A cry echoed from the black depths, and Matt realised that unless whoever was making the noise came out now, they were going to need a torch before they could explore any further.

'Hello?' Jo called.

The cries became more agitated but no one appeared. They ventured in a little way and called again.

'I'll go and buy a cheap torch,' Jo volunteered. 'I'm a faster runner than you.'

Matt was not going to argue. He delved into his jeans pocket and found a few pound coins.

'I have some money too,' said Jo, grabbing them and stuffing them into her pocket. Then she was off, sand spraying behind her heels, and he was left standing alone, wondering whether to stay and talk to whoever was trapped in the cave, or get well back from the cliff.

His instinct of self-preservation won.

CHAPTER SIX

Jo came back, panting, carrying a smallish torch.

'It was the biggest I could get for the money we had,' she explained, seeing Matt's expression. 'I had to buy batteries too, don't forget.'

The roof of the cave sloped downwards but then continued at a height of about two metres. It was sandy underfoot and strewn with seaweed. Matt wasn't sure why, but that made him uneasy. He was busy concentrating on the crying sound, still coming from further in.

They clambered over a rocky outcrop, through a small tunnel that led them into a bigger space. They could hear water trickling, though they couldn't see it. Matt shivered, fully aware of the risk they were taking.

'Helloooo?'

Each time they called, they were answered, but Matt was beginning to doubt that the cry was human.

Then they saw it: a small black and white dog, wedged between two rocks. It wagged its tail when it saw them, and whined.

Matt ran forward.

'Be careful,' warned Jo, for once being the less impulsive one.

Jo placed the torch on a rock, so that it shone onto the dog. First they tried to move one of the rocks that was trapping it, but they were deeply embedded in the sand. In fact, Matt and Jo soon realised that they were probably only the tops of bigger rocks, like icebergs.

'Maybe we should try to lift him out,' suggested Jo.

She took firm hold of its hindquarters, avoiding the dog's head. Matt moved over to reassure the dog. He stroked it for a minute or two and then gently grasped its front end. He looked over at Jo, and together they lifted.

The dog came out easily, and shook itself before doing a little prance around them.

'Now we have to find the owner,' said Matt.

Jo was waving the torch around the cave. 'Hey! There's some writing on the wall.' She concentrated the beam on one spot and walked closer to it.

'Graffiti,' said Matt. 'Come on.'

'No, wait! It's a rhyme. It's about revenue men.'

'Revenue men?'

'You know! It's what they used to call customs men.'

Matt went over to stand beside her. 'But that was ages ago.'

The writing was etched into the rock wall and some parts had weathered away, but it was still legible.

Into this rocky hollow
You revenue men do follow
Entry only at low tide
What better place to hide?

Too late! I am gone! No trace!
You'll have to try another place.
I pray, Sirs, that I'll be forgot
For to catch me you shall not.
IG

'Smugglers!' said Jo.

Matt smiled and shook his head. 'You've been reading too much Enid Blyton.'

'No, it must be!' she insisted. 'They used to hide the booty somewhere until it was safe to get it away. What better place than a cave?'

Matt had to admit, it was interesting, but he

pretended indifference. 'Come on, let's get out of here.'

They returned through the narrow section; the dog followed after them. Matt would have expected it to scamper out ahead of them, but it seemed reluctant to leave the cave.

Then he saw why.

The tide had come in.

CHAPTER SEVEN

They both stared at the water that had crept up the beach and into the cave. The sea was still a bit choppy from the previous night's storm and each wave, fringed with foam, swirled in aggressively.

'I never thought of the tide,' said Jo.

'I didn't either,' admitted Matt, 'although we should have known when we saw seaweed on the cave floor.'

'But it's shallow. It's no problem.'

'Well, the dog's not going,' Matt observed. 'They have an instinct for these things. We don't know what the currents are like round here.'

'Don't be silly.' Jo began pulling off her trainers. 'It can't be that deep.'

Matt watched as she stepped boldly into the

water, then grabbed for his hand as she was nearly swept off her feet. She looked at him and smiled ruefully.

'You're right. Not a good idea.'

'I wonder how far up the tide comes.' Matt looked back into the cave. It did slope upwards, but not very much.

'Hey!' Jo brightened. 'If this cave was used by smugglers, it must lead somewhere. They needed to get it inland and away.'

Matt waited while Jo tried to dry her feet and smiled when she pulled a face as she put her damp feet back into her trainers.

They clambered back into the cave where they

had found the dog and then shone the torch into the dark depths beyond. The dog had already run on ahead.

There was a tunnel at the back of the cave that climbed steadily upwards, quite steeply at times. Matt wondered how the smugglers would have carried their hoard, but it depended on what they were smuggling, he supposed. Bottles of brandy would have been a struggle. He didn't bother to mention it to Jo. She would know, of course, and he would seem ignorant. Dinosaurs were what he knew about.

Neither of them mentioned the constant sound of gurgling water as it trickled between the rocks and earth all around them. Matt imagined all the rain they had had gradually seeping down to sea level, turning earth to mud as it went. He glanced at the walls around them worriedly. They looked solid enough, but then again, so did cliff faces ... until they fell. He was afraid to voice his thoughts in case it proved bad luck.

The tunnel became very narrow and they had to crawl through, until they were almost wriggling on their bellies. Matt felt his stomach sink in fear as the walls closed in claustrophobically.

'How did men ever get through here?' Matt asked.

'Weren't people smaller in those days?' Jo replied.

Matt knew she would have an answer.

'In which days?'

He imagined her shrug, but couldn't see Jo as she was behind him.

'Whenever the smugglers were from.'

The dog was way ahead, obviously anxious to get out as soon as it could too. Where was this going to lead? To a dead end? Somewhere long since bricked up or blocked by erosion and rock falls?

The end came suddenly. There was no light at the end of the tunnel. It just ended.

Matt and Jo were silent for a moment. Was she also imagining the tide creeping up behind them? But Matt knew it couldn't reach them up here. It wasn't possible, was it? The feeling of being trapped made him feel breathless, as if he was already short of air.

Then Jo banged on the wall. It sounded oddly hollow.

'It's wood!' She looked round for something to bang it with, and picked up a small rock.

Matt did the same and they began to pound on

the wooden wall, hoping it had rotted with age and damp.

It shook a little, but held firmly, obviously made of hardwood. In annoyance and half in panic, Matt gave it a push.

It moved. It actually wobbled.

'I think it's something standing there, like some heavy furniture,' said Jo, panting with the effort.

They both gave it all they had. Suddenly, the wooden object teetered forward, paused for a moment, and then crashed down. There was the sound of glass breaking as well as the wood.

Matt and Jo stepped into what looked like a cellar. Big barrels were lined up around the walls, and they weren't full of brandy. Bits of broken bottles were strewn over the floor.

'It's a pub!' said Matt. 'Those are barrels of beer and ale.'

The landlord of *The Ship Inn* was very surprised to see two dishevelled and damp children and a dog emerge through the cellar door and Matt found it difficult to make a long story short. The customers listened in awe at the news of the secret tunnel.

Jo was eager to quote the verse on the wall. 'Was there a smuggler with those initials?'

Matt hurriedly said, 'Well, it was probably just

written by kids mucking about …' It would be better to check it out at the museum before getting too excited, though Matt had a feeling that the landlord would be bricking up the entrance more permanently very soon. In fact, the murmurings amongst the locals showed a strong leaning towards blocking up the entrance to the cave, too, to prevent others getting cut off by the tide. The lifeboat service had already been called out twice this week to rescue people, not to mention the ever-present danger of rock falls and landslides.

'Best not tell anyone,' said the landlord.

Matt looked at Jo. Who did he think they were going to tell? They didn't know anyone here.

As soon as they emerged from the pub the dog started to trot, very purposefully, up the road. They

followed the dog up the hill and turned right, where it stopped outside a whitewashed cottage and barked.

Just as Matt and Jo reached the house, the door opened and an elderly man came out. He saw the dog and smiled broadly.

'Brian!' he exclaimed, bending down to fondle the dog's head. He looked up.

'Where did you find him?'

'He was stuck … in between some rocks on the beach,' said Jo.

The man shook his head. 'He should have been a cat, he's so curious! Thank you very much. We were on a walk and he just ran off. I thought he might find his way home on his own.'

'Well that was a happy ending,' said Jo as they left.

'Look at you!' said Mum when they reached the house. 'What on earth have you been doing?' But Matt didn't want to give her the whole story. Not right now, anyway.

'Did you find any fossils?'

Jo delved into her pocket. 'Just one ammonite.'

Mum laughed.

'Where's Dad?'

'Oh,' she said, 'there's been a big find on the beach so they came to fetch him.'

'A big fossil find?' said Matt. How come they had missed it? They'd been there, right on the spot, but somehow hadn't seen anything going on. 'How did they know Dad was here?'

Mum smiled. 'You know your dad. Don't you remember he introduced himself at the museum yesterday?'

But Matt was already on his way to the door, followed very closely by Jo.

He was not going to miss out on this, and Mum knew better than to try to stop them.

CHAPTER EIGHT

A crowd had gathered on the beach to the west of the town, the opposite direction to the way Matt and Jo had gone earlier. Despite the high tide and the brisk wind, people squinted towards the cliffs, seeming almost to hold their breaths in anticipation.

There'd been a recent landslide. You could tell because the exposed earth and rocks looked fresh and damp. It looked as though a massive chunk of the cliff had fallen.

Dad was standing near the top of the huge heap, about ten metres up, bending over to examine something. A couple of men were huddled next to him, but most of the crowd was standing well back on a level part of the beach that was still above the high tide mark.

'I wonder what it is,' said Jo. 'I hope it's something new.'

Matt was hoping the same thing. He longed to go up and join his father but knew they'd send him back. It was far too dangerous up there: there was no way of knowing whether more of the cliff face was about to fall. Dad and the other men would be working as quickly as possible to make sure they weren't near the cliff any longer than necessary. Distractions were the last thing they needed. Nevertheless, Matt inched forward whenever someone moved away. If only he could see what was going on …

Suddenly there was a commotion. Matt heard Jo gasp and looked around. Frank Hellman's big frame was pushing through the crowd, bulldozing everyone out of the way.

'Let me through. I'm a palaeontologist!' he said, loud enough for everyone near him to hear.

'There's a palaeontologist already up there!' someone shouted. 'It's Mr Alan Sharp.'

Frank Hellman's only response was to give a swift shake of his head and then he began to climb the debris, scrambling on hands and knees. He was about halfway up when Matt's dad must have heard something because he turned around and saw Hellman. He frowned, and said something to him that Matt couldn't hear.

What can he say, Matt thought, *in front of all these people? He can't appear to be angry that there is another palaeontologist on the scene. People would expect them to be colleagues.*

He and Jo exchanged glances, both wondering what would happen next.

What did happen was surprising.

Frank Hellman did himself no favours by appearing to elbow Dad out of the way as he looked down at the find. When Dad stood his ground, Hellman looked around, and then bent and picked up a big rock.

Jo gasped and Matt could feel his heart thumping. Surely he wasn't going to attack Dad in front of everyone?

The crowd was hushed, mesmerised by the drama being enacted in front of them. They had come to see a dinosaur unearthed and hadn't expected a display of such animosity.

But it wasn't Dad who was Hellman's target. Matt could see now that he was intent on smashing the fossils. Dad had said before that Hellman had no real interest in palaeontology, but could never live up to his own father's expectations of him. Frank Hellman just

wanted the prestige that was bestowed on great scientists.

His first blow echoed back from the cliffs and sent a shock wave radiating through the crowd. Everyone seemed to take a step back, but then they all surged forward again for a better look.

The second blow was stopped in its tracks as Matt's dad grabbed Hellman's arm in mid-air. But Hellman was a big man and he broke free, almost causing Mr Sharp to lose his balance. Then Hellman dropped the rock and threw a punch at Dad, who fell back onto the rubble. Matt couldn't believe what he was seeing and he felt so helpless.

'Matt!' Jo's face had an expression of horror as she turned to look at him. 'This can't be happening.'

Would no one stop this?

Then, as the two men grappled with each other, the men who had been up there examining the find with Dad decided to do something. They each grabbed one of Hellman's arms and half clambered and half slipped down the rock fall, still holding on to Hellman. Matt could see his red angry face and gritted teeth and he gave a howl of anger, trying to free himself.

The two men marched Hellman through the crowd, which parted like the Red Sea, and only when they were well clear of the area did they let him go with a little push. A small cheer went up and the previous silence was filled with chatter now.

Matt heaved a sigh of relief and caught Jo's eye and smiled.

'Best entertainment anyone here has had in a long time,' he said. 'That Frank Hellman is really serious.'

'I think we knew that already,' said Jo.

Attention was back on the three men on the heap of rubble. Matt was aware of the danger his dad and the other men were in. So much for Dad's advice to stay away from the base of the cliffs.

'I know what you're thinking,' said Jo, in that uncanny way she had of mind-reading. 'But Mary Anning risked her life every day gathering fossils to sell on her stall. It's how she made money to help to feed her family.

Matt nodded. He wondered what it was that had been found up there. It looked as though Dad and the others were trying to remove the piece of rock containing the fossil. Surely they wouldn't be able to lift it. Mary and her brother had spent weeks carefully extracting the fossils from the rock. Nowadays they could bring in some machinery to lift it and take it to a more pleasant place to do the careful chiselling.

Some of the crowd was beginning to drift away now that there was nothing much to see. It wasn't the best weather to be standing about. Matt wondered whether there was any point in him and Jo staying there, either.

He looked up at the cliff looming above. It was sheer rock for thirty or forty metres.

Suddenly a movement caught his eye. A figure up on top. What madness to stand up there when the ground could break away at any moment! Especially after all the rain last night and the recent landslip.

Then he thought he recognised the figure. There was something about the shape of it, the shaven head, the frenzied way it was busy up there. Doing what?

'Jo!' Matt felt sick. 'Frank Hellman is up on top of the cliff. I think he's going to cause something to fall on Dad.'

CHAPTER NINE

'Matt! We have to warn your dad.'

Matt was well aware of that, but since the fracas between Dad and Hellman, those people who hadn't drifted away seemed to be discussing it loudly. Before, they had been intent on the find, now the noise level had risen, and what with the cries of the seagulls and the sound of the sea, Matt knew that Dad would never hear them call.

Matt and Jo did call out, though, as loudly as they could, but Matt could hear the wind whip away his words as soon as they left his mouth.

They pushed forward through the crowd, earning some angry words, but politeness was unimportant now. Dad's life was at stake.

No one else had spotted the figure on the cliff top and, as they made their way forward, Matt lost sight of him too. But Hellman was still there, he knew, and not being able to see him was even more worrying. What was he doing up there?

'Dad!'

But his father couldn't hear him. He was too engrossed in trying to ascertain which rocks were to be removed with little damage to the bones.

Matt's heart was pounding and he felt hot, despite the cold wind. The plaintive screech of the seagulls added to his feeling of helplessness and doom. He wished these people would realise what was happening.

At last they reached the foot of the landslide.

'Dad!'

Now Mr Sharp seemed to hear. He stood up and looked down at the crowd, searching for Matt.

Just then Matt saw a little dribble of soil and rocks begin to slide down the sheer cliff face. Like an avalanche, it grew in speed and volume. At the same time a huge crack appeared in the cliff and a block of earth the size of a house teetered.

It was like watching something in slow motion.

'Dad!' Matt and Jo pointed up at the cliff top. 'Landslide!'

As Dad looked up and saw it, so did the crowd. Like a frightened shoal of fish they scattered, some screaming. Matt and Jo ran too, all the time looking over their shoulders.

Dad and the other two men threw themselves to the side.

With a thunderous noise the chunk of cliff hit the beach, spraying out earth and terrifyingly massive rocks.

Matt felt earth scatter on his back but fortunately no rocks. They had just managed to get out of range.

Despite the rain, dust hung in the air making it difficult to see anything around the pile of debris.

Without thinking, Matt began to scramble up the heap.

'Hey! You kids! Come back,' someone yelled.

'My dad!' cried Matt. 'My dad's up there.'

Some people joined them then, and a couple of people started shouting for someone to call an ambulance. There was no sign of Dad or anyone else. Matt felt tears sting his eyes as he made frustratingly slow progress towards the spot where he had last seen his father.

'Stay here, we'll look for them.' Two men overtook Matt and Jo. But Matt shook his head. They had done enough standing and watching. He had to go and help.

The dust choked up his throat making him cough, and he could hear the rasping sound his breathing made as he struggled up the last few metres to the top of the landslip, followed closely by Jo. He was so glad that she was there too. It was good to have someone sharing his anxiety; someone who loved the man buried under the rubble almost as much as he did.

Then Dad appeared gradually out of the rubble looking like an apparition. He just rose from the earth, covered in chalky dust, brushing down his clothes, and Matt wondered for a moment whether he was real or whether there *were* such things as ghosts.

'Matt! Jo!' The ghost felt very solid as it embraced them both in a strong grip. 'You two shouldn't be up here.'

Matt said nothing, but just hugged his dad.

'You all right, mate?' asked one of the men who had come up to search.

Dad nodded. 'You'd better check the other two, but I'm certain they're fine too.' Then he looked round, searching the ground. 'What a nuisance. We've got to dig those fossils out again!'

What an understatement. It made Matt smile briefly, but then he was serious again. 'It was Frank Hellman, Dad,' he said. 'He started the landslide. We saw him up on top of the cliff just before it happened.'

'What?' Dad looked appalled. 'I can't believe he would stoop to …'

'Murder?' said Jo. 'We should tell the police, Uncle Alan.'

Matt's dad sighed. 'And tell them what? We have no proof except what you say you saw.'

Matt nodded. 'And they won't believe us.'

His dad looked resigned. 'Look, Matt, everyone here saw the confrontation we had, and although Hellman was obviously the aggressor, people wouldn't believe the differences between us could be so strong.'

People helped them down and crowded round, sympathetically. An ambulance had arrived and the paramedics insisted in checking the three men caught in the landslide. Dad had a few abrasions but had luckily escaped injury.

'Let's get back to the house,' he said. 'Your mum will be worried.'

Matt and Jo kept quiet about their exploits. Matt was not sure they needed to tell his parents anything. One person putting themselves in danger was enough for one day.

CHAPTER TEN

The fossils were surprisingly undamaged when they dug them out of the rubble over the next few days. Matt's dad and several other enthusiasts, armed with a mechanical digger, worked hard. It was an ichthyosaurus, just like the one that Mary and Joseph Anning had found when Mary was twelve. *Same age as me*, Matt thought.

'What about eggs, Dad?' he said, when the bones had been transported to the museum and they were all back at the house.

His dad smiled. 'You're not likely to find any of those.'

'Why not?'

'Ichthyosaurs didn't lay eggs; they gave birth to live young.'

Matt remembered the drawing. 'Have you ever heard of a geologist called Henry De la Beche, Dad?'

His dad stared at him. 'Henry De la Beche? Of course. He was an eminent geologist as well as the first palaeo-artist. Did you read about him in the museum?'

Matt went to get the drawing, unrolling it in front of his dad, who gasped and looked up at him, astonished. 'Where did you get this?'

'We found it in the cellar hidden behind a loose brick.' Matt didn't mention the vision he'd had. The drawing was enough for now.

Carefully, Mr Sharp took the paper from Matt and smoothed it out as though it were about to shatter into pieces. 'What I wouldn't give to own this!' he said.

'But you can, Dad.'

His dad stared at him, then shook his head. 'No, it belongs in a museum where everyone can enjoy it.'

'But we found it in this house, Uncle Alan,' said Jo.

'And this isn't our house, Jo. Come to think of it, it must have been Mary Anning's house as an adult, given that you found this drawing in the cellar. She didn't stay in the house of her birth all her life.'

'Wow!' Jo looked at Matt. 'Amazing!'

There was just one more thing left for them to do. They paid another visit to the museum and Jo asked the curator if she knew of a smuggler with the initials IG.

'Of course! Isaac Gulliver. He was infamous around here in the 18th century.'

'What did he smuggle?'

'Oh, tea,' she said. 'The tax on tea was very high then so that only the rich could afford it. Also lace and silk. Sometimes spirits.'

Tea, silk and lace, thought Matt. Those he could

have easily hauled up the tunnel. Perhaps not the spirits though.

'Our last day here tomorrow,' said Matt as they walked back up the hill to the house.

'I know what I'm going to do,' said Jo, surprising him.

'What?'

'There's going to be a litter drive. A beach clean-up. We have to meet on the beach at eight o'clock and we'll be given gloves, rubbish bags and grabber things. It'll be low tide then.'

'Count me out,' said Matt. He couldn't think of anything less fun.

'I never counted you in,' Jo laughed.

As they turned towards the house, Matt looked up at it. 'To think that Mary Anning lived here,' he said. 'They should put a plaque on the wall.'

As he looked down to turn in to the short path he gave a gasp and bent down to pick up one of the rocks that were placed either side of the entrance.

Jo stared as the realisation dawned on her too. 'So she did excavate it but maybe never realised what it was.'

Matt's head was going fuzzy.

He was on a beach again, similar to before, but there was no scelidosaurus there now. Suddenly he felt a wind on his face and heard the sound of wings flapping. He looked up just as a huge prehistoric flying reptile swooped down.

Matt ducked instinctively, although it couldn't see him.

This was a pterosaur with a wingspan of over a metre. It landed a few metres in front of him and he could clearly see its huge head and beak resembling a puffin's. At the end of its long, pointed tail was a diamond-shaped flap.

The dimorphodon (Matt was certain that's what it was) made its ungainly way towards the edge of the sea, its sprawled-out legs giving it an awkward gait. Swiftly, it plucked at something, which Matt then saw was a fish, tilted its head in the air, and chomped down hard. Unlike birds, it had teeth.

'Matt! Are you all right?'

It was Dad. Jo had fetched him and his mum and Beth. They all stood around him on the short path.

The egg became heavy in his hand and he gently laid it on the ground, although it was certainly not going back to mark the gateway. He glanced at the other rock, and was certain that's all that one was. Just a rock.

Then he smiled up at his family.

'Dimorphodon egg,' he said. 'There it was all the time. We passed it every day.'

'Well spotted,' said Dad. 'So at least we won't go home empty-handed.'

'But Frank Hellman will,' said Jo.

Author's note: Some of the geographical features of Lyme Regis I've mentioned in this book are real, but others are fictional. To my knowledge, there is no tunnel between the beach and a pub cellar, but the infamous smuggler, Isaac Gulliver, was real, so who knows?